The
Panicosaurus

The Panicosaurus

Managing Anxiety in Children Including Those with Asperger Syndrome

Written by K.I. Al-Ghani

Illustrations by Haitham Al-Ghani

Jessica Kingsley *Publishers*
London and Philadelphia

First published in 2013
by Jessica Kingsley Publishers
116 Pentonville Road
London N1 9JB, UK
and
400 Market Street, Suite 400
Philadelphia, PA 19106, USA

www.jkp.com

Library of Congress Cataloging in Publication Data
A CIP catalog record for this book is available from the Library of Congress

British Library Cataloguing in Publication Data
A CIP catalogue record for this book is available from the British Library

ISBN 978 1 84905 356 3
eISBN 978 0 85700 706 3

Printed and bound in China

This book is dedicated to
Ahmed and Sarah Al-Ghani
for their continued love and support.

Acknowledgements

I would like to give a special thank you to Bryony Gladwish, who chose some of the character names in the story and discussed the contents of the book with great honesty. Also to Lynda Kenward, Ashlie Linfield and Audrey Norcross, whose vast experience with children means I can turn to them for advice as well as friendship.

Introduction

Anxiety can occur when the demands placed on us by our environment are out of harmony with our ability to cope with them. An area in the brain called the amygdala is responsible for the sensations we experience at these times. When anxiety takes hold, we cannot control these sensations – they happen automatically, without conscious thought. When we experience an emotion like fear our body responds by making us breathe faster, which in turn sets the heart racing. We can react to this fear and anxiety in a number of ways, known as "The Five Fs":

1. FLOCK: This is when we go to trusted people who help us to feel safe (for example, Mum, Dad or the police) or when we head for a crowd (safety in numbers!).

2. FLUSTER: This is when we start to panic and make silly mistakes because we can't seem to think straight (remember that driving test?).

3. FREEZE: This is when we are caught like a rabbit in the headlights, unable to move or speak.

4. FLIGHT: This is when our automatic reaction is to run away at the fastest possible speed.

5. FIGHT: This is when we become agitated, angry and aggressive.

The amygdala is also implicated in the storage of memories; indeed, I once heard it described as the "storehouse of the memory of fear." When memories are negative, we may come to equate certain situations with strong emotions. This could be a fear of the dark, of dogs or of the dentist, for example. Left unchecked, this fear can become overwhelming and it is often difficult to persuade an individual that there is no real danger, especially when the body is subconsciously telling them that there is.

Most young children, no matter how much we try to protect them, will experience some moments of fear and anxiety. For overly anxious children, however, it is important that we teach them to recognise, and therefore reduce, the uncomfortable symptoms they may be feeling at these times. These children need opportunities to practise calming techniques at times when they are least stressed. By giving them automatic and positive responses to use when a situation becomes frightening or overwhelming, we are arming them with key tools to use throughout life.

A proactive approach involves teaching children strategies that will help them learn how to control feelings of panic through relaxation and visualisation. If, by using these methods, we can reduce anxiety and lead the child to a more peaceful place, we will have succeeded in giving them some control over their fears. If we can also induce gentle laughter – that most exquisite of mental releases, peculiar to humans – it will be an added bonus. It is thought that the first human laughter may have started as a gesture of shared relief at the passing of danger. The relaxation that results from smiles and genuine laughter inhibits the fight-or-flight response and so is a valuable tool to help to control anxiety, especially in children, although it should never be forced. Interestingly, in some children with autism uncontrollable laughter may actually be a sign of acute anxiety.

For children with autism spectrum disorder (ASD), anxiety is something they may have to struggle with on a daily basis. Children with autism, especially those with Asperger syndrome, seem to worry excessively about everyday events that typical children would normally take in their stride. The correlation between autism and anxiety was memorably described by Dr Tony Attwood when he said that "Autism is anxiety looking for a target."

It is believed that a dysfunctional amygdala may contribute to the abnormal rates of fear and anxiety that seem to be a common feature of ASD. A large percentage of children (and adults) with ASD have what is known as alexithymia, which is difficulty in identifying feelings. When they are upset they may be unable to say whether they are sad, frightened or angry. Combined with this, many people with ASD have additional sensory sensitivities that can create a feeling of anxiety, the most common being an aversion to certain sounds or unexpected noises. Children with autism seem to be hypervigilant; that is, they are constantly on the lookout for threatening situations. These children are often unable to find coping skills to help them deal with the demands of everyday living. In a busy mainstream classroom, for example, any change in routine, such as the absence of a trusted member of staff or the unexpected clanging of the fire bell, may result in a feeling of acute anxiety or a panic attack. The build up of anxiety caused by these stressful situations is likely to eventually lead to an extreme response. The child may run out of the classroom or the school building; he or she may become non-compliant, aggressive or argumentative; or may find somewhere to hide (in my many years observing children in schools, a favourite hiding place is often under the table).

Neuroscience teaches us that if you want to change a behaviour, you need to practise the response. For example, you cannot just tell a person how to drive a car. They need to be taught and then given time to practise the skills involved until, finally, driving becomes almost automatic. The same principles apply to stress and anxiety – children need to be given the opportunity to practise techniques that will help them to reduce their feelings of panic.

Practising relaxation techniques at regular intervals throughout the school day could prove very effective in managing the build-up of anxiety in the child. The story of the

Panicosaurus can enable children to visualise anxiety in such a way that they will recognise the symptoms and learn ways to control their fear. Read to a whole class, the story can help other children to become more sympathetic towards an anxious child. It can also alert parents and professionals to the responses they should show when a child has withdrawn out of fear and anxiety (they may make the incorrect assumption that the child is attention seeking or simply using an avoidance tactic to get out of doing something they dislike).

Read by a parent or professional to an individual child, the story of the Panicosaurus can give anxious children a chance to talk about their own feelings and express a desire to help themselves in a more positive and soothing way. The story makes it clear that anxiety is an emotion shared by everyone and controlled by our brains. It is the way we deal with these emotions that really matters to our personal well-being.

The techniques suggested in this book can be taught to a whole class, not just the anxious child. Indeed, we can all benefit from knowing what to do when that Panicosaurus pounces!

Deep inside everyone's brain is a place called the amygdala (pronounced am / ig / duh / luh).

A little dinosaur called the Panicosaurus lives in the amygdala. The Panicosaurus used to be kept very busy in the days when people lived in caves.

He had the very important job of warning the cavemen about danger. Perhaps a sabre tooth tiger was on the prowl or a hairy mammoth was trying to push his way into the warm cave.

Panicosaurus would help the caveman by getting his brain to tell his body to breathe faster, so that his heart would beat more quickly and pump extra oxygen to the muscles in his legs and arms. This meant the caveman would be ready to run like the wind or fight for his life.

These days, however, the Panicosaurus is frightfully bored. Dangerous creatures no longer roam the places where people live and work. In some people, the Panicosaurus is happy to be lazy and will only pounce if a mouse should scuttle by, or if a spider is hiding in the bath or a slithery snake is lurking in the long grass.

In other people, the Panicosaurus is rather mischievous. He can make them feel afraid, even when there is nothing to be afraid of!

How many times have you felt the presence of the Panicosaurus? In the dark, perhaps? Maybe when visiting the dentist or the doctor? Does he show up when you have to take a test or talk in front of the class?

When the Panicosaurus pounces he can make us breath more quickly so, just like the caveman, our hearts beat faster and we may feel some very uncomfortable sensations. We may feel hot and sweaty or cold and clammy, our knees may knock, our hands may shake, our mouths may go dry, the hairs on the back of our necks may stand up and our tummies may feel full of a thousand butterflies.

The Panicosaurus is frightfully good at filling our minds with thoughts of danger and he can make us worry about silly things. In most people, the Panicosaurus is kept in check by another little dinosaur called Smartosaurus.

Smartosaurus lives in a part of our brain called the neocortex. If we listen to him, he can tell us when Panicosaurus is playing tricks. He can help us think about our breathing and control the strange sensations our bodies may be feeling.

Smartosaurus has clever ways of getting Panicosaurus to behave himself. However, in some people (especially children) Panicosaurus finds it easier to be naughty. Smartosaurus must work extra hard to get him to stop playing those nasty tricks that make children feel fearful and anxious.

This is the story of a very naughty Panicosaurus and a little girl called Mabel Green…

It was a crisp Monday morning in May. Mabel Green was feeling especially happy because after school that day she would be going to the toy shop with Mummy to buy a new picture puzzle. Mabel had earned her puzzle by learning how to sleep right through the night.

Ever since she could remember, Mabel had been afraid to go to bed. As soon as Mummy or Daddy covered her up with the quilt and kissed her goodnight, Mabel's breathing would quicken, her heart would start thumping in her chest and she would feel hot and sweaty. She didn't know why, but her head would be full of a whole bunch of "What if...?" questions:

"What if Mummy and Daddy go out?"

"What if I am all alone in the house?"

"What if there are monsters hiding in the cupboard?"

These pesky questions would frighten Mabel so much that she would throw back her quilt, jump out of bed and flip on the light.

Then, one restless night, Daddy told Mabel all about the Panicosaurus. He told her that she did not have to listen to the Panicosaurus – she could learn to listen to the Smartosaurus instead.

Smartosaurus told Mabel there was no danger, it was just Panicosaurus playing tricks because he was bored. If she wanted Panicosaurus to go away, she must first learn to do some deep breathing.

Learning how to breathe properly was easy when Mabel lay on her tummy. She could feel the air filling her chest. Daddy trained Mabel how to breathe in deeply on a count of 2, 3, 4 and then blow out the breath saying:

"PANIC-O-SAURUSSSSSSSSSS."

This slowed down Mabel's breathing; her heart would stop racing and Panicosaurus would begin to lose his power over her.

As soon as Mabel had learned how to breathe properly, Daddy devised a plan. He promised he would come into Mabel's room every five minutes to check on her. Mabel had to promise to try to stay in bed and concentrate on her breathing to blow out that Panicosaurus.

The first time they tried it, five minutes seemed like a very long time so Daddy said not to worry, they would try for two minutes. Little by little, as Mabel practised her breathing, she built up to fifteen whole minutes, and then she fell fast asleep!

Daddy bought her a little torch that looked like a penguin (her favourite creature) so that, instead of getting out of bed to put on the light, she could flick on the torch and tell the Panicosaurus to "Go away!" because everything was okay.

Each morning after a successful sleep, Mabel was given some tiddlywinks to put in a jar, and when she had collected enough she would get a picture puzzle. Mabel was working on getting enough tiddlywinks for a thousand-piece puzzle.

On the way to school one morning Mabel got into a panic. Coming down the street towards her was a dog. Panicosaurus told her that dogs bark, dogs bite, dogs are dangerous! Mabel felt like she wanted to run, but Mummy had fast hold of her hand. "What did Smartosaurus tell us to do? Take a deep breath and sing!"

"Dogs are loyal, dogs are true, (to the tune of "Hush Little Baby")

If they are on a leash, they won't bother you.

Look at his tail, does it wag as he walks?

No need to listen to that Panicosaurus talk."

Smartosaurus knew that Panicosaurus hated singing – it stops his power almost immediately. Mabel took a deep breath, blew out the Panicosaurus and sang along with Mummy. Before they could say "bow-wow" the dog had passed by and Mabel smiled. "Gosh Mabel, that was fantastic! I'm putting twenty-five tiddlywinks in your jar just as soon as I get home," said Mummy proudly.

Mummy left Mabel at the school gate.

"Enjoy your day, darling, see you after school. Remember, we are going to the toy shop!" she reminded Mabel encouragingly.

Mabel used to be afraid of the playground and she would often start crying when the time came for Mummy to leave. One time she even ran after Mummy into the busy road and almost got knocked over by a car. So with the help of the Smartosaurus Mummy devised a cunning playground plan to fight off that pesky Panicosaurus.

On the playground there was a big green circle. It was Mabel's Green Spot. When the Panicosaurus threatened to surface Mabel would run to stand on her spot, reach into her bag and bring out the bottle of bubbles that she always carried with her. Taking a deep breath she would blow out the bubbles and all the children would charge around her trying to pop them without stepping on the green spot. The laughter of the excited children kept Panicosaurus at bay. Smartosaurus knew that Panicosaurus couldn't bear to hear laughter, it just saps him of all his power.

Soon it was time to go indoors, and in the bustling cloakroom Mabel could not find the peg with her name under it. She scanned the rows of pegs, but her name was not there. A sense of panic swept over her as Panicosaurus whispered in her ear.

"What if this is not your school?"

"What if the children don't know you?" he challenged.

One of the classroom assistants, Mrs White, noticed the anxious look on Mabel's face. Taking her by the hand she led Mabel to her peg. As they walked, she sang:

"We're off to find our peg,

We're off to find our peg,

E-I the al-E-O we're off to find our peg."

Mabel noticed that the name card had fallen down onto the floor. Mrs White bent over to pick it up and helped Mabel to fix it back in place. Mabel smiled gratefully at Mrs White.

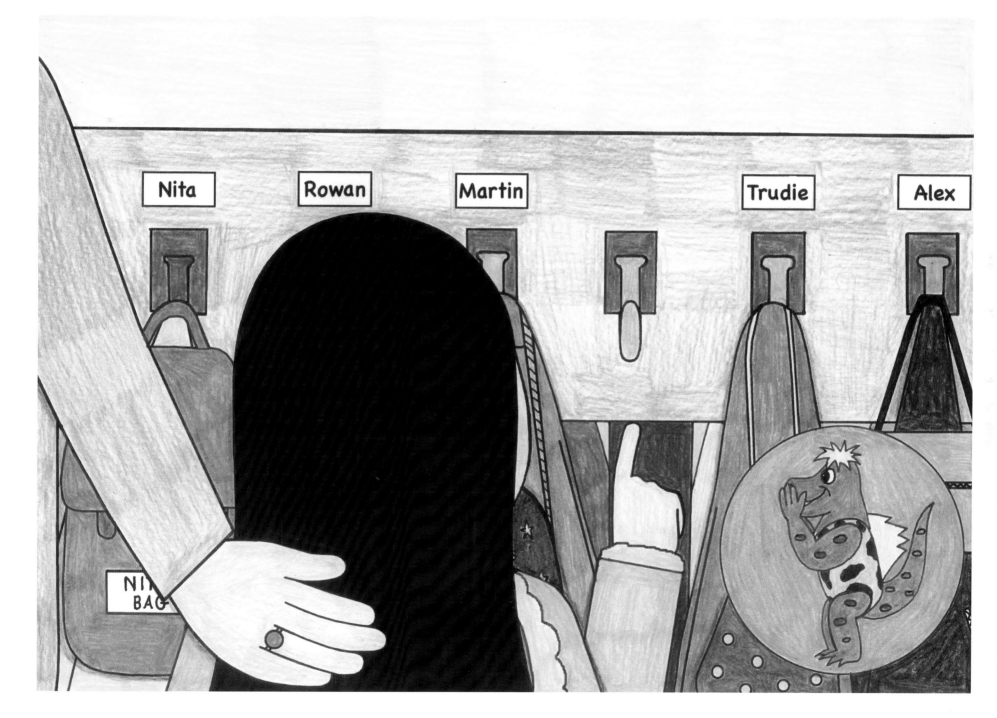

In the classroom the children took their seats, but Mabel couldn't see her teacher, Mrs Pink. Where was she? Perhaps *she* had fallen down like the name card, Mabel joked to herself. Before she had time to ask one of her classmates about Mrs Pink, the door opened and in walked a tall, young man.

"Good morning, children," he called out, "My name is Mr Grey. I'll be your teacher for today because Mrs Pink is not feeling very well," he explained to them kindly.

After the incidents with the dog and the label in cloakroom, this change to Mabel's day was all it took to make the Panicosaurus particularly bothersome. Mabel sprang out of her seat and scrambled under the table like a frightened rabbit.

Mrs Pink was Mabel's favourite teacher and pink was her favourite colour. She could not possibly like anyone with a name that was the colour grey!

Mr Grey began to call out the register, but when he got to Mabel's name there was no reply.

"Where is Mabel?" Mr Grey asked the class.

"Under the table," chanted the children.

"Under the table?" echoed Mr Grey, in disbelief. "Mabel Green, get out from under that table at once!" he ordered sternly.

The children looked at each other anxiously.

"Erm, it's all right, Mr Grey," explained a girl called Trudie Bell, rather nervously, "Mabel sometimes goes under the table when she feels afraid."

Mr Grey raised his eyebrows and carried on calling the register.

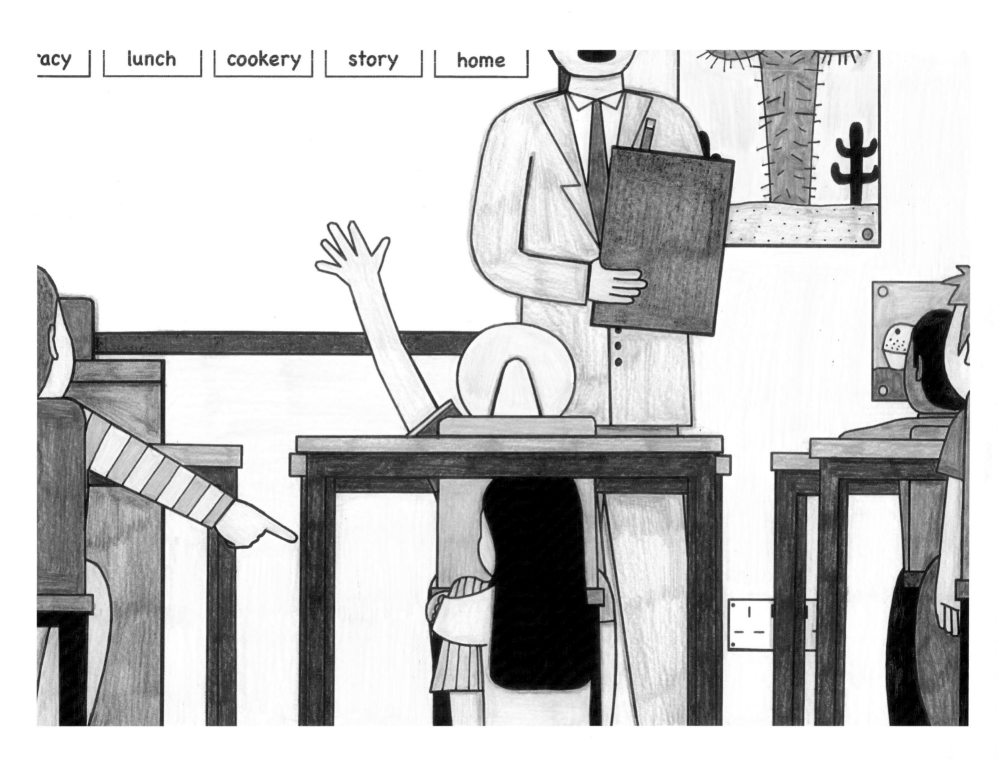

Under the table Mabel was battling with the Panicosaurus.

*"What if Mr Grey does not let you do your puzzle
at lunchtime?"* Panicosaurus goaded.

Mabel remembered what Mrs Pink had taught her. Taking a deep breath she clenched her toes tightly and pushed her feet hard into the ground. Then she breathed out slowly whispering "Panic-o-saurussss."

Taking another deep breath she squeezed her legs together tightly, then she breathed out slowly saying "Panic-o-saurussss." A third deep breath meant Mabel must push her palms together as hard as she could, then out came the breath with a "Panic-o-saurussss."

Mrs Pink had told her to throw those "What if…?" questions right back at the Panicosaurus. So Mabel said defiantly, "What if Mr Grey is a lovely, kind teacher who knows all about my puzzle-making at lunchtime?"

"What if you just go away and leave me alone!"

Panicosaurus slunk back into the amygdala and Mabel crept out from under the table and sat in her chair.

The children were greatly relieved when they saw Mabel back in her seat and they gave her the "thumbs up" sign. Mabel began to relax. Soon the morning was over and it was time for the children to line up for lunch.

Usually, after lunch Mabel returned to the classroom to work on her jigsaw puzzle. Today it was Martin Brown's turn to stay in class and keep her company. Mabel was looking forward to the afternoon lessons. It was always cookery on a Monday. This week they were going to make a witch's pot full of vegetable soup. All the children had been told which vegetables to bring in and they were going to take some of the soup home for tea. Mabel was going to prepare the carrots.

Mrs Pink had asked the children to think up a little rhyming couplet to say as they added the vegetables to the pot. Mummy had helped Mabel to think of one and she was going to say:

"When the soup is bubbling hot,

Put the carrots in the pot."

When Mr Grey returned to the classroom, he moved the arrow along the timetable and then he replaced the "cookery" symbol with a "painting" symbol.

"No, no, that cannot be right!" thought Mabel, beginning to feel funny inside. Mrs Pink had promised they would make vegetable soup, and she had carrots waiting to be chopped and added to the pot.

"I'm sorry children," explained Mr Grey, "I'm afraid I don't have the necessary equipment with me to do cookery, so I think we will do some painting instead."

All the children were disappointed, but this further change to Mabel's routine was just too much to take and she became distraught. Her eyes filled with tears, her hands began to shake and her tummy felt painful. Before Mr Grey could say anything more, Mabel was under her table, head in her arms, sobbing.

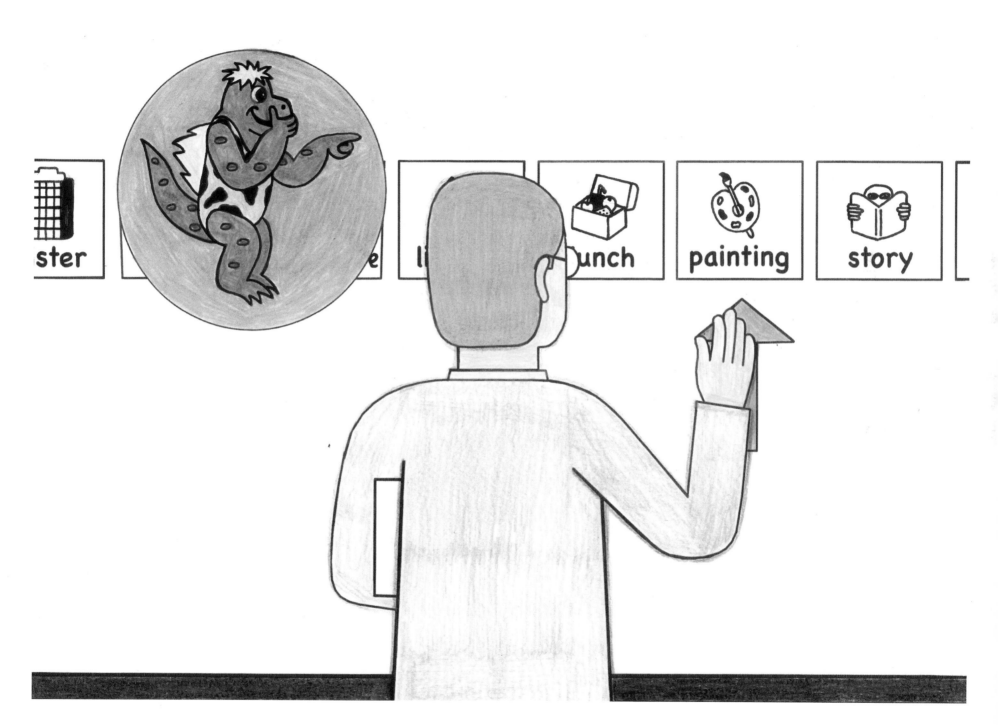

"Where's Mabel?" asked Mr Grey with concern. But he knew the answer — she was back under the table.

All the children in the class looked so sad as they heard Mabel's sobs. Trudie asked if she could go into Mrs Pink's cupboard. Once there, she found a large box with Mabel's name on it and inside she found a blanket, a stuffed penguin, a torch and Mabel's "The Silly Panicosaurus Book."

Trudie quickly threw the blanket over the table and gently pushed the lighted torch into Mabel's "den," together with the penguin and the book. Then she softly repeated Mrs Pink's mantra:

"I feel calm,

I feel safe,

I am happy in this place."

Taking her stuffed penguin in her arms, Mabel picked up the torch and opened "The Silly Panicosaurus Book." It was filled with pictures of the Panicosaurus looking quite ridiculous. Mrs Pink had set the class a challenge to draw the Panicosaurus but to make him look very funny.

There was Panicosaurus dressed like a clown; Panicosaurus in a funny hat with cross-eyes; Panicosaurus in a nappy with a baby's bottle and a comforter in his mouth, and many, many more. Mabel could not help herself and she started to smile.

Slowly, a little corner of the blanket was lifted and Mr Grey gave Mabel a heated pad that smelled of lavender. Mabel held it to her tummy and she began to relax.

Trudie gave her a beaker of water with a fitted straw and Mabel took a sip and then, slowly but surely, she began to feel calm.

After about half an hour, Mabel was ready to come out. Blinking in the light of the afternoon sun, she sat down in her chair and looked around the room. Trudie smiled at her and gave her the "thumbs up" sign.

Mabel enjoyed painting and she decided that she would paint a picture of some penguins, so everything was going to be okay. Trudie put Mabel's special things away in her relaxation box.

At the end of the school day, Mr Grey had a quiet word with Mabel's mother (she usually took Mabel home five minutes before the rest of the school went home) and they found a special story in the relaxation box, which explained that sometimes teachers were ill and a substitute teacher would be in charge of the class. Mrs Green said she would read it with Mabel that night when she was ready for bed.

Just before home time, Mr Grey thanked Mabel's class for all their help, especially Trudie. He told them that he had learned a great deal that day and he would be sure to tell Mrs Pink what a fine class of caring children she had.

To show his appreciation, he was going to bring them a class pet – a little hamster named Buster! He showed the children a picture of Buster and they all cheered. They felt proud and happy as they left for home that day.

Meanwhile, after picking up her new picture puzzle from the toy shop, Mabel was relieved to reach home. It had been a hard day as the Panicosaurus had been so troublesome.

However, Mabel was confident that she could control that naughty creature whenever she needed to. By listening to the Smartosaurus she was already well on the way to getting that puzzle with one thousand pieces!

Strategies to reduce stress and anxiety

🐾 Discuss what happens to the body when we become distressed. For example, we may feel shaky, nervous, nauseas, sweaty or have a dry mouth. We may feel like we want to run away and hide or we may become very agitated, angry or aggressive. Children could list things that make them feel this way, for example:

- public speaking

- a visit to the dentist, doctor or hospital

- spiders

- snakes.

🐾 Teach the children relaxation techniques like simple deep breathing (also known as diaphragmatic breathing). Breathe in deeply on a count of 2, 3, 4 then breathe out on a count of 2, 3, 4.

🐾 Use muscle tensing then relaxing – as Mabel does in the story. Start with the feet and work your way up through the major muscles of the body, exaggerating the exhale with a big "AHHHHHHHH" or "PANICOSAURUSSSSSSSS."

🐾 Promote positive self-talk, such as "I am calm," "I am relaxed," "I feel peaceful," "I feel safe." Children can think up their own mantra (a mantra is an expression or idea that is closely associated with something – in this case, a feeling of well-being – and is repeated often without thinking about it).

🐾 Prepare a peaceful place, for example a wigwam or a tent in a corner of the room (this may be better than going under the table). Give the child a card to show or put in a designated place when they need to go to their retreat.

- Make relaxation fun! Try yoga or Tai Chi (you may be lucky to have a parent or colleague who is proficient in one of these ancient arts and may be persuaded to come into school to demonstrate it to the class). Some children may find that an energetic activity, such as trampolining, is a more effective and enjoyable way for them to relax and let go.

- Promote happy thoughts. Make a "Happy Scrap Book" filled with favourite images or make your version of "The Silly Panicosaurus Book," or play a favourite cartoon on a DVD player away from the rest of the class.

- Regularly practise relaxation before transition times (for example, when going out to play, at lunch time, home time, etc.). The class could enjoy a few quiet moments with their heads down and eyes shut. The teacher could spray the room with a favourite fragrance (check the child with ASD likes the smell first!) or play some soothing classical music. This is a good routine to put in place at the start of every school day.

🐾 Have younger children teach a favourite soft toy how to relax and how to breathe properly.

🐾 Teach children how to give themselves a butterfly massage. Get the children to start at their heads and flutter their fingers over their hair, face and shoulders, then cross over their arms and flutter down each arm. When they get to their hands, they should grasp each finger one by one and tug gently, then rest their hands on their stomach and do some deep breathing. Tell them to imagine the butterfly flying away with all their worries.

🐾 Tell children to give themselves a big hug by crossing their arms over their chest and squeezing firmly.

🐾 Keep a relaxation diary. Chart the frequency of the practice and note which exercises work well.

🐾 Make a stress level thermometer for the child to indicate how stressed or fearful they are on a scale of 1 to 5.

🐾 Show children how to do a chin push, by interlocking their fingers and placing their hands under their chin, then pushing down on the hands before relaxing.

🐾 Prepare a box of sensory toys, such as squeezy things, lava lamps and LED displays. You could also use lavender blankets, scented heated pads or weighted jackets (check the child with ASD has no aversions to these items first).

🐾 Have the children plant seeds and be responsible for a little patch of garden.

Finally, as parents it is important that we remain calm when children are showing signs of stress. I find it helps to think of oneself as a boat. We need to be on an even keel, stable and solid, if we are to be supportive to the anxious child.

Preventative strategies for the child with ASD

🐾 Enlist the help of an occupational therapist to put together a set of exercises to aid deep muscle relaxation and have the child practise these at regular intervals throughout the school day and at home.

🐾 Help the child to become desensitised to noises or places they may find difficult. This can be done by playing the noise or going to the difficult area over a period of time, starting with a very short time and gradually increasing it.

- Rearrange school times so the child can avoid overcrowded areas like the cloakroom or playground. Allow the child to come into school five minutes early and leave five minutes early. Let the child choose whether they'd prefer to stay in the classroom over playtime or eat lunch with a friend instead of in a busy (and often smelly) dining hall.

- Whenever possible prepare the child for any changes to routine by using pictorial narratives or Social Stories™.

- Reward typical children when they are sympathetic towards the anxious child and when they give up their own playtimes or lunch times to befriend them.

- Reward the anxious child when they try to overcome their fears.

- Provide a transition toy for a small child to hold whenever they need to move from one activity to another. This can be kept at school (this is better than having the child bring in a beloved toy that may get lost or broken or be used inappropriately).

19 ⁹⁵